W9-BGP-396

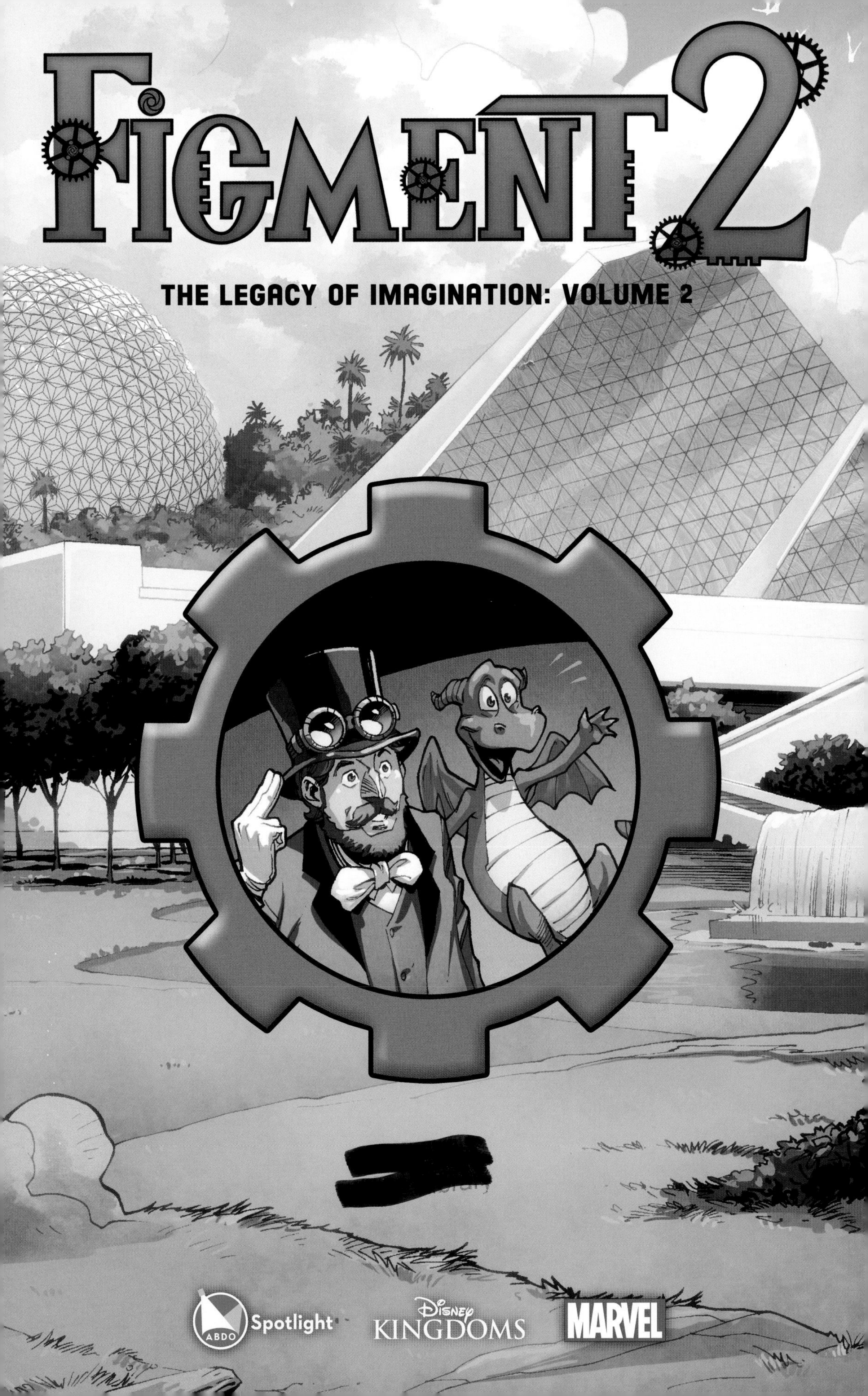
FIGMENT 2
THE LEGACY OF IMAGINATION: VOLUME 2
[redacted]
ABDO Spotlight
DISNEY KINGDOMS
MARVEL

ABDOPUBLISHING.COM

Reinforced library bound edition published in 2017 by Spotlight,
a division of ABDO, PO Box 398166, Minneapolis, Minnesota 55439.
Spotlight produces high-quality reinforced library bound editions for
schools and libraries. Published by agreement with Marvel Characters, Inc.

Printed in the United States of America, North Mankato, Minnesota.
092016
012017

THIS BOOK CONTAINS
RECYCLED MATERIALS

marvelkids.com
© 2015 MARVEL

Elements based on Figment © Disney.

PUBLISHER'S CATALOGING IN PUBLICATION DATA

Names: Zub, Jim, author. | Bachs, Ramon ; Beaulieu, Jean-Francois, illustrators.
Title: Figment 2 : The Legacy of Imagination / writer: Jim Zub ; art: Ramon Bachs
    ; Jean-Francois Beaulieu.
Description: Reinforced library bound edition. | Minneapolis, Minnesota : Spotlight,
    2017. | Series: Disney Kingdoms : Figment Set 2
Summary: After flying through a portal, Dreamfinder and Figment find themselves
    in the 21st century at the new Academy, but when a demonstration goes
    wrong, Dreamfinder transforms into the Doubtfinder, leaving Figment and
    Capri to free Dreamfinder before doubt can take over the world.
Identifiers: LCCN 2016941716 | ISBN 9781614795810 (volume 1) | ISBN
    9781614795827 (volume 2) | ISBN 9781614795834 (volume 3) | ISBN
    9781614795841 (volume 4) | ISBN 9781614795858 (volume 5)
Subjects: LCSH: Disney (Fictitious characters)--Juvenile fiction. | Adventure and
    adventurers--Juvenile fiction. | Comic books, strips, etc.--Juvenile fiction. |
    Graphic novels--Juvenile fiction.
Classification: DDC 741.5--dc23
LC record available at https://lccn.loc.gov/2016941716

Spotlight

A Division of ABDO
abdopublishing.com

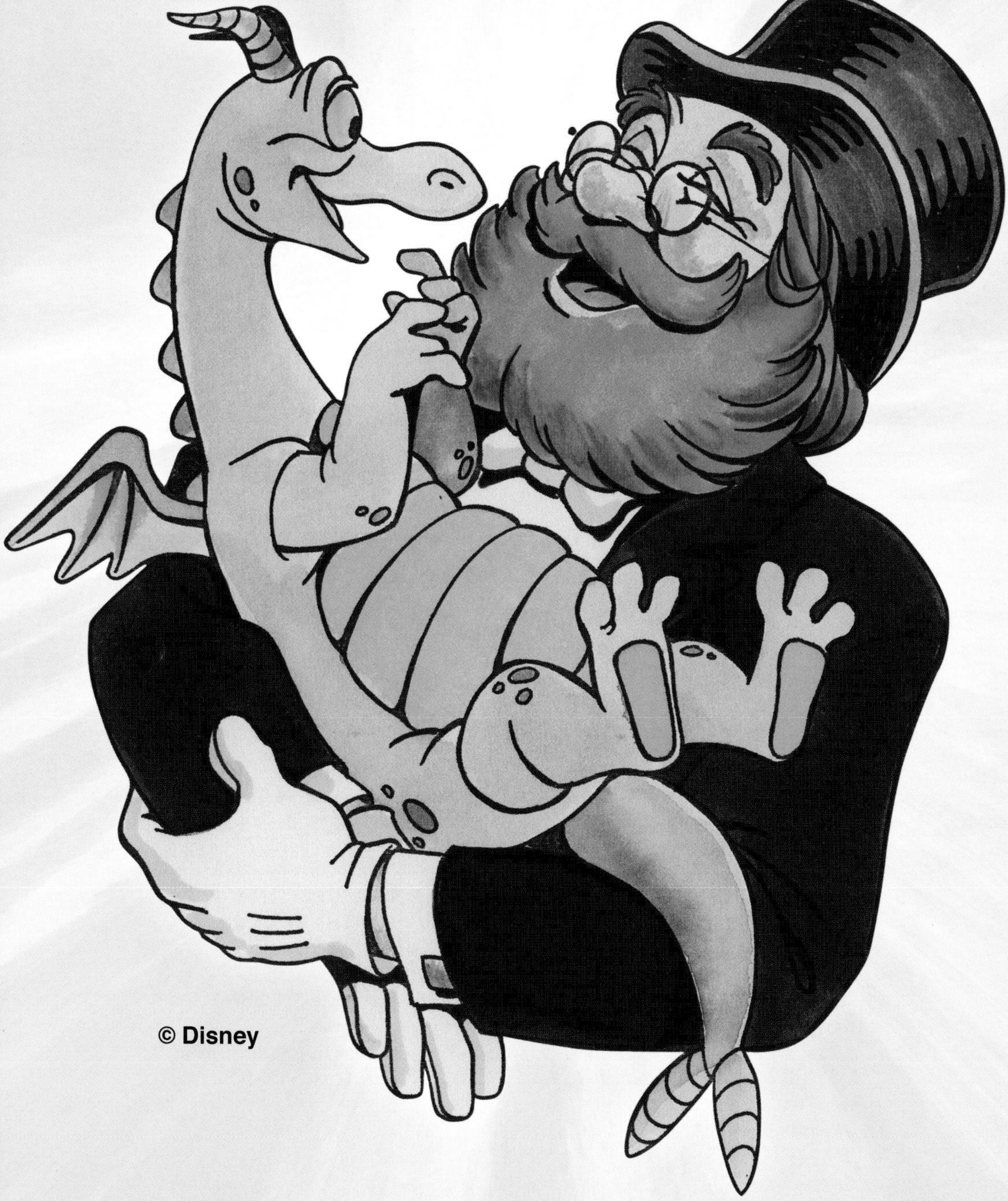
© Disney

Early Figment and Dreamfinder character designs for the Journey Into Imagination ride by X Atencio

Artwork courtesy of Walt Disney Imagineering Art Collection

FIGMENT 2

A century ago, a young inventor at the Academy Scientifica-Lucidus created a being called **Figment** using his newly designed, thought-powered machine: the Mesmonic Converter. Soon after, the machine pulled them into a dreamlike world where they visited realms of pure imagination, leading Blair to reach his full creative potential and become the **Dreamfinder**. They returned home in time to save the planet from a destructive force accidentally unleashed with the converter in their absence.

In taking down the threat, the duo piloted their flying Dream Machine through a portal where they came upon a mysterious geodesic sphere. They landed their malfunctioning airship to discover they'd traveled to the 21st century location of the new Academy, run by **Chairman Auckley**, who immediately assumed them to be reckless imposters intruding on his school. **Fye**, the sound sprite they met on their first journey into imagination, is now a professor at the school and was able to vouch for them. Auckley was not yet convinced, but arranged for a school demonstration of the power of imagination. Only, Dreamfinder's not quite sure he can live up to the legend that's grown around him in the intervening 100 years...

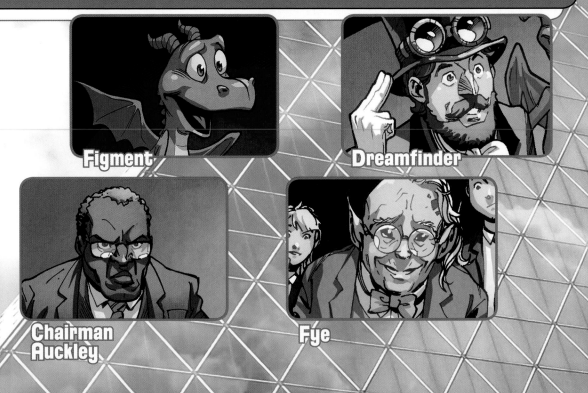

Figment

Dreamfinder

Chairman Auckley

Fye

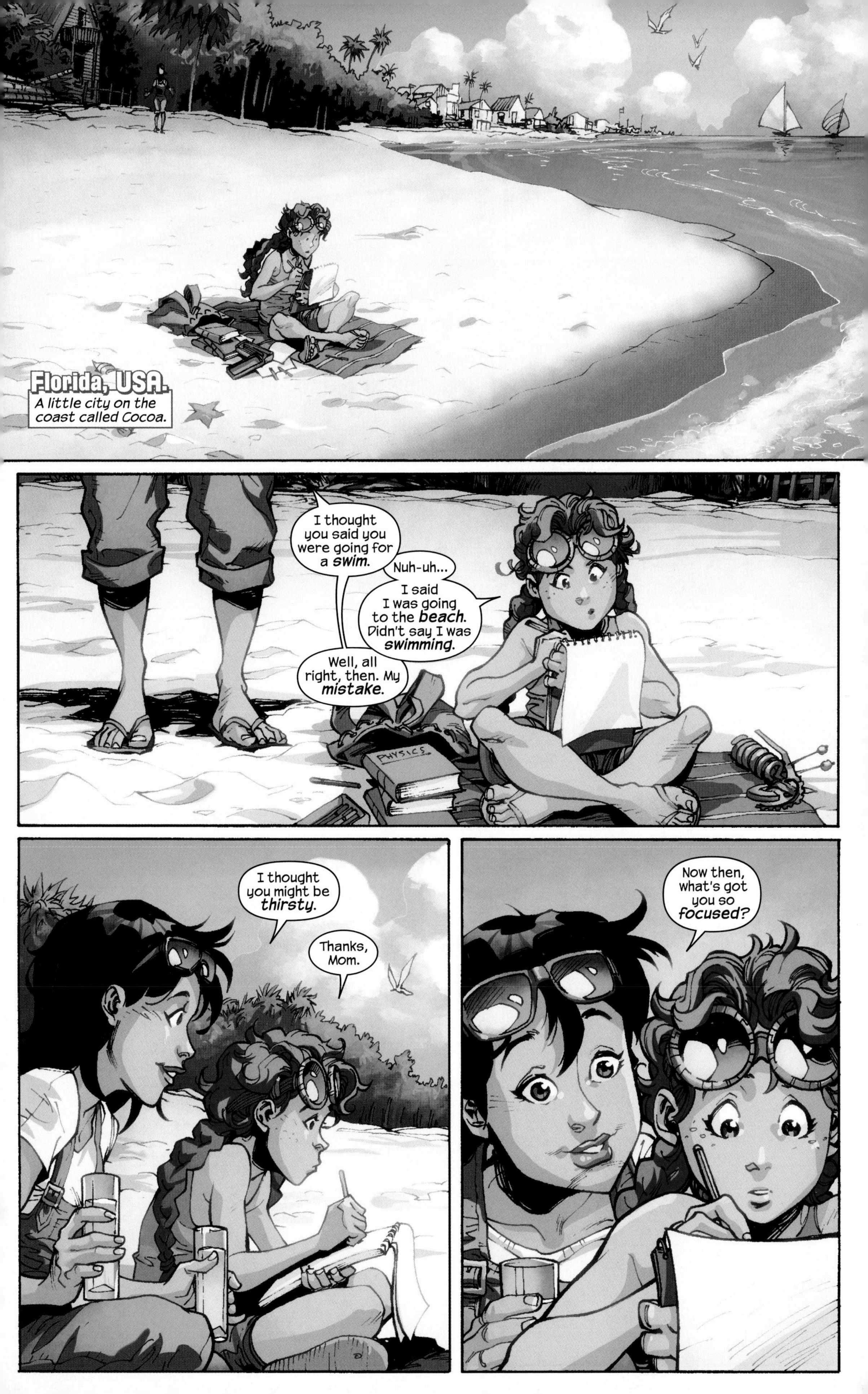
Florida, USA.
A little city on the coast called Cocoa.
I thought you said you were going for a swim.
Nuh-uh...
I said I was going to the beach. Didn't say I was swimming.
Well, all right, then. My mistake.
PHYSICS
I thought you might be thirsty.
Thanks, Mom.
Now then, what's got you so focused?

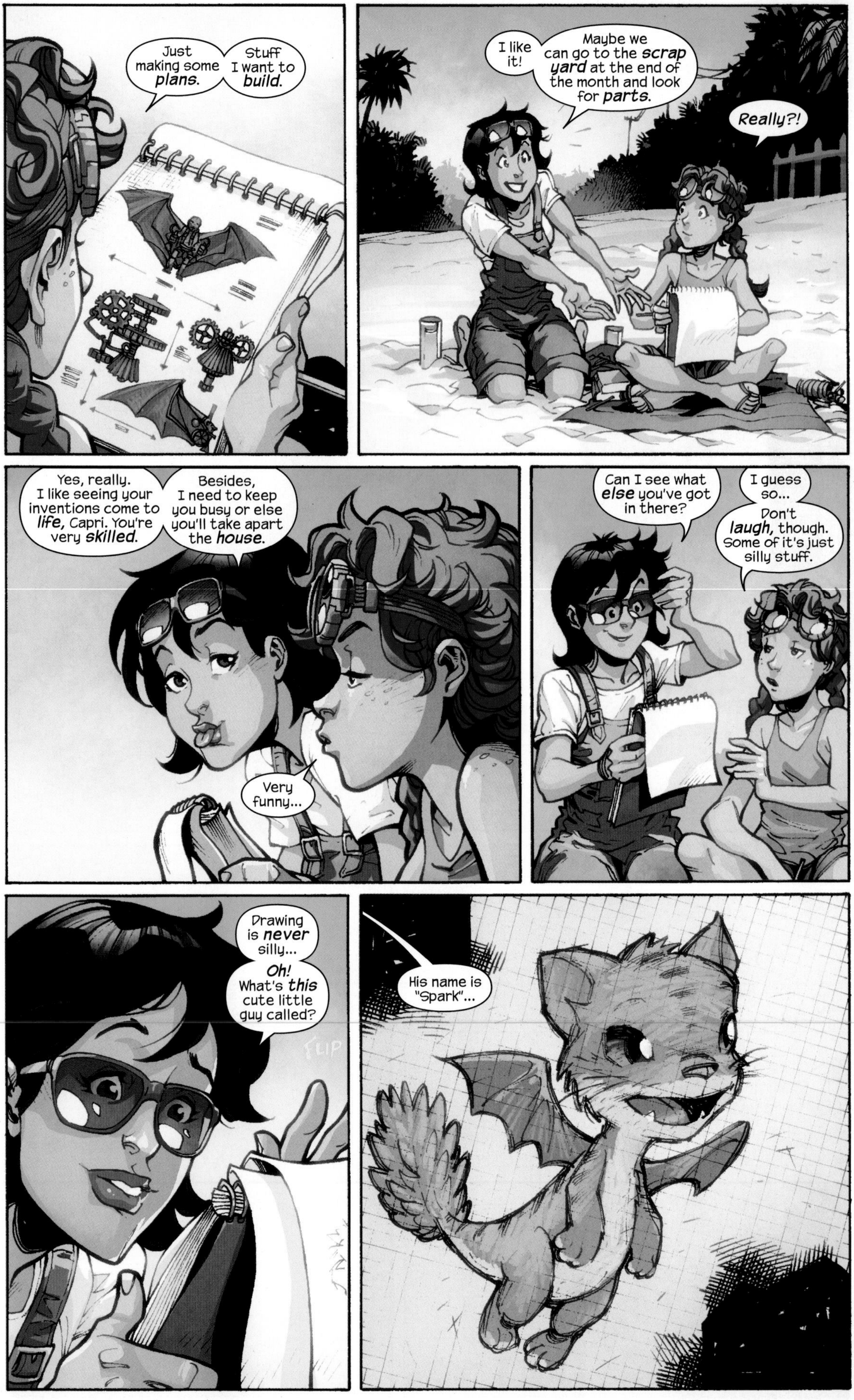
Just making some *plans*.
Stuff I want to *build*.
I like it!
Maybe we can go to the *scrap yard* at the end of the month and look for *parts*.
Really?!
Yes, really. I like seeing your inventions come to *life*, Capri. You're very *skilled*.
Besides, I need to keep you busy or else you'll take apart the *house*.
Very funny...
Can I see what *else* you've got in there?
I guess so...
Don't *laugh*, though. Some of it's just silly stuff.
Drawing is *never* silly...
Oh! What's *this* cute little guy called?
FLIP
His name is "Spark"...

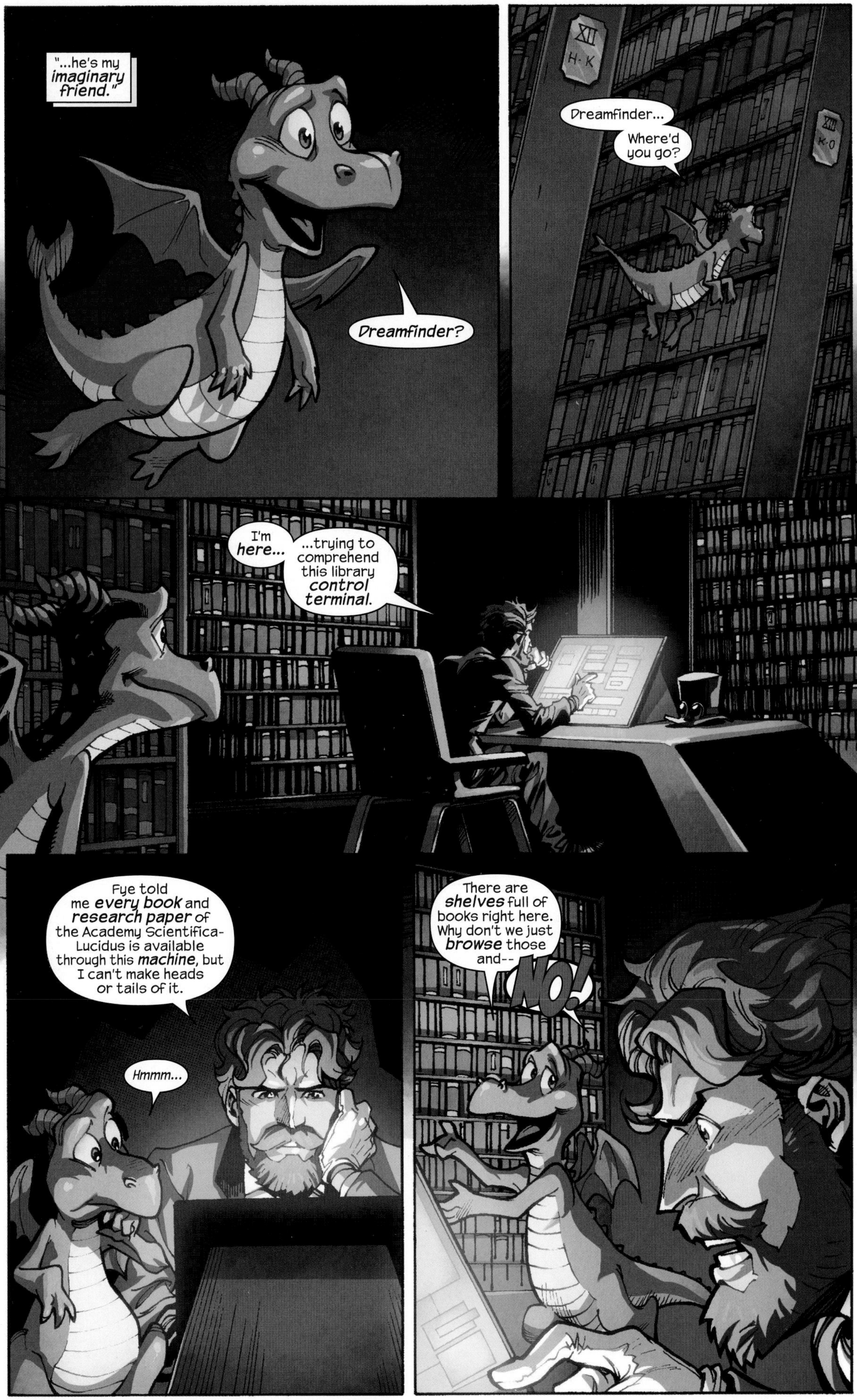
"...he's my imaginary friend."
Dreamfinder?
Dreamfinder...
Where'd you go?
I'm here...
...trying to comprehend this library control terminal.
Fye told me every book and research paper of the Academy Scientifica-Lucidus is available through this machine, but I can't make heads or tails of it.
Hmmm...
There are shelves full of books right here. Why don't we just browse those and--
NO!

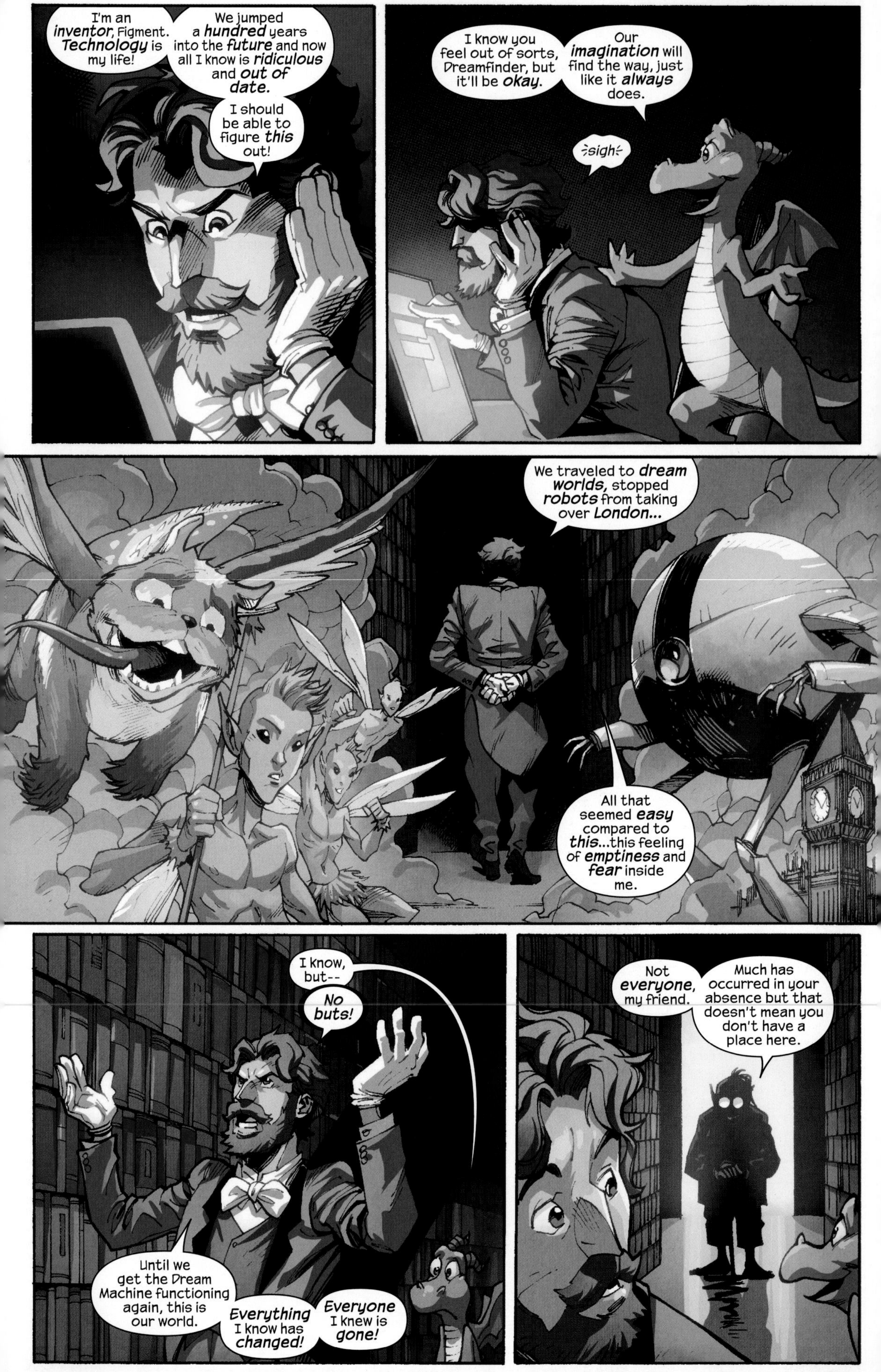
I'm an inventor, Figment. Technology is my life!
We jumped a hundred years into the future and now all I know is ridiculous and out of date.
I should be able to figure this out!
I know you feel out of sorts, Dreamfinder, but it'll be okay.
Our imagination will find the way, just like it always does.
sigh
We traveled to dream worlds, stopped robots from taking over London...
All that seemed easy compared to this...this feeling of emptiness and fear inside me.
I know, but--
No buts!
Until we get the Dream Machine functioning again, this is our world.
Everything I know has changed!
Everyone I knew is gone!
Not everyone, my friend.
Much has occurred in your absence but that doesn't mean you don't have a place here.

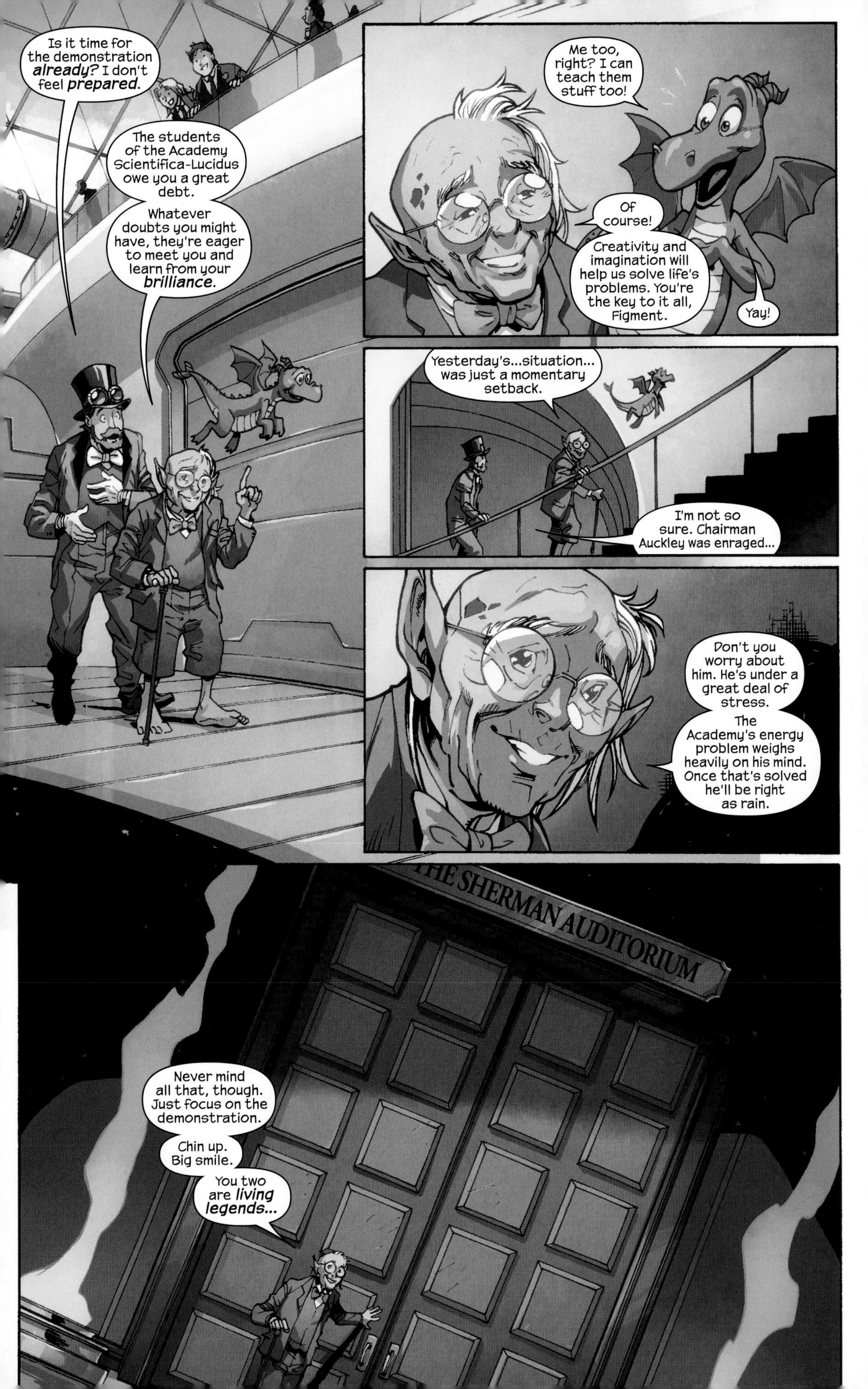
Is it time for the demonstration *already?* I don't feel **prepared**.
The students of the Academy Scientifica-Lucidus owe you a great debt.
Whatever doubts you might have, they're eager to meet you and learn from your ***brilliance***.
Me too, right? I can teach them stuff too!
Of course!
Creativity and imagination will help us solve life's problems. You're the key to it all, Figment.
Yay!
Yesterday's...situation... was just a momentary setback.
I'm not so sure. Chairman Auckley was enraged...
Don't you worry about him. He's under a great deal of stress.
The Academy's energy problem weighs heavily on his mind. Once that's solved he'll be right as rain.
THE SHERMAN AUDITORIUM
Never mind all that, though. Just focus on the demonstration.
Chin up. Big smile.
You two are *living legends...*

The Legacy Of Imagination
Part Two: Rising Doubts
JIM ZUB writer
RAMON BACHS artist
JEAN-FRANCOIS BEAULIEU colorist
VC's JOE CARAMAGNA letterer
...so show them what you've got!
Wowie-WOW!

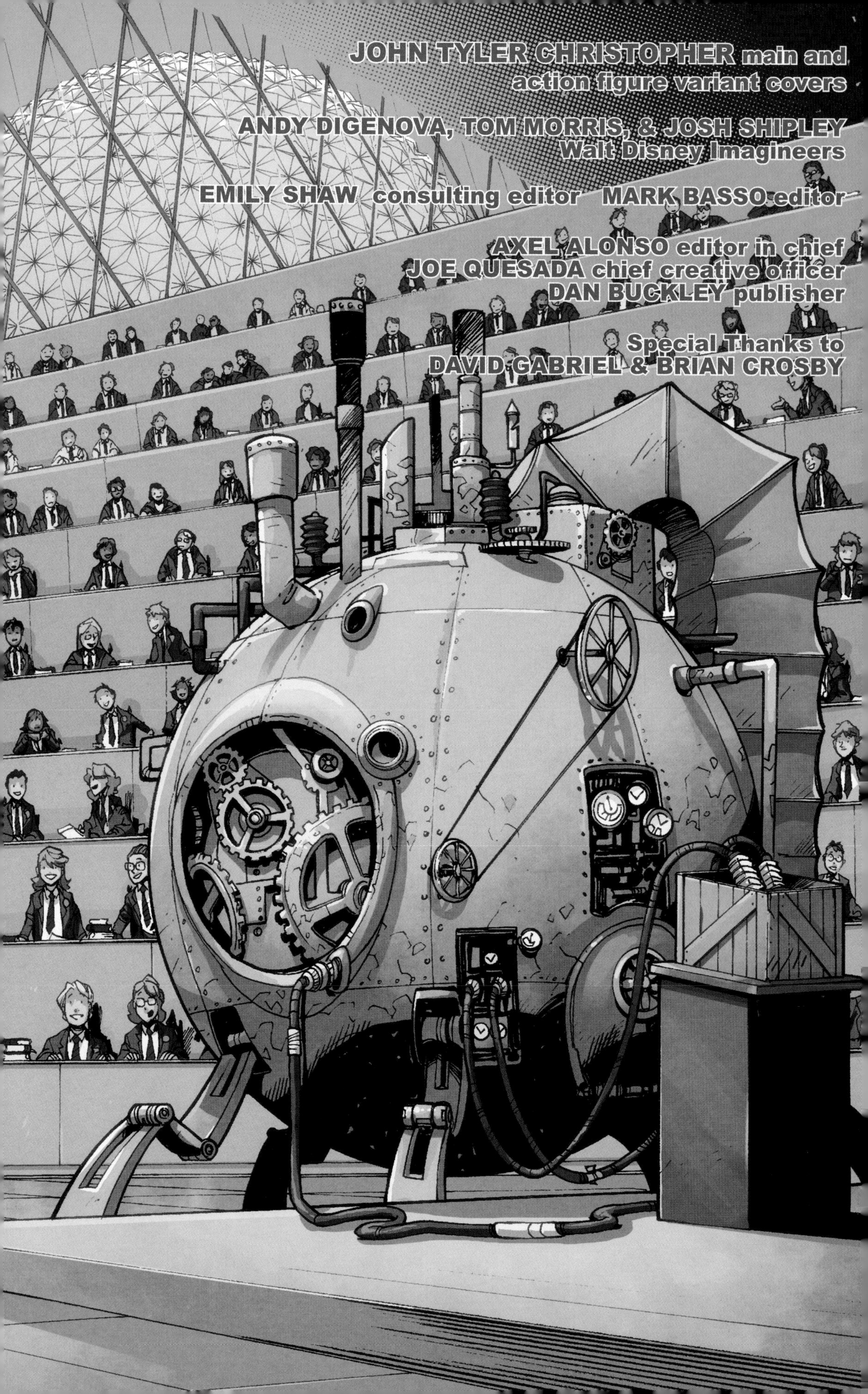

JOHN TYLER CHRISTOPHER main and action figure variant covers

ANDY DIGENOVA, TOM MORRIS, & JOSH SHIPLEY
Walt Disney Imagineers

EMILY SHAW consulting editor **MARK BASSO** editor

AXEL ALONSO editor in chief
JOE QUESADA chief creative officer
DAN BUCKLEY publisher

Special Thanks to
DAVID GABRIEL & BRIAN CROSBY

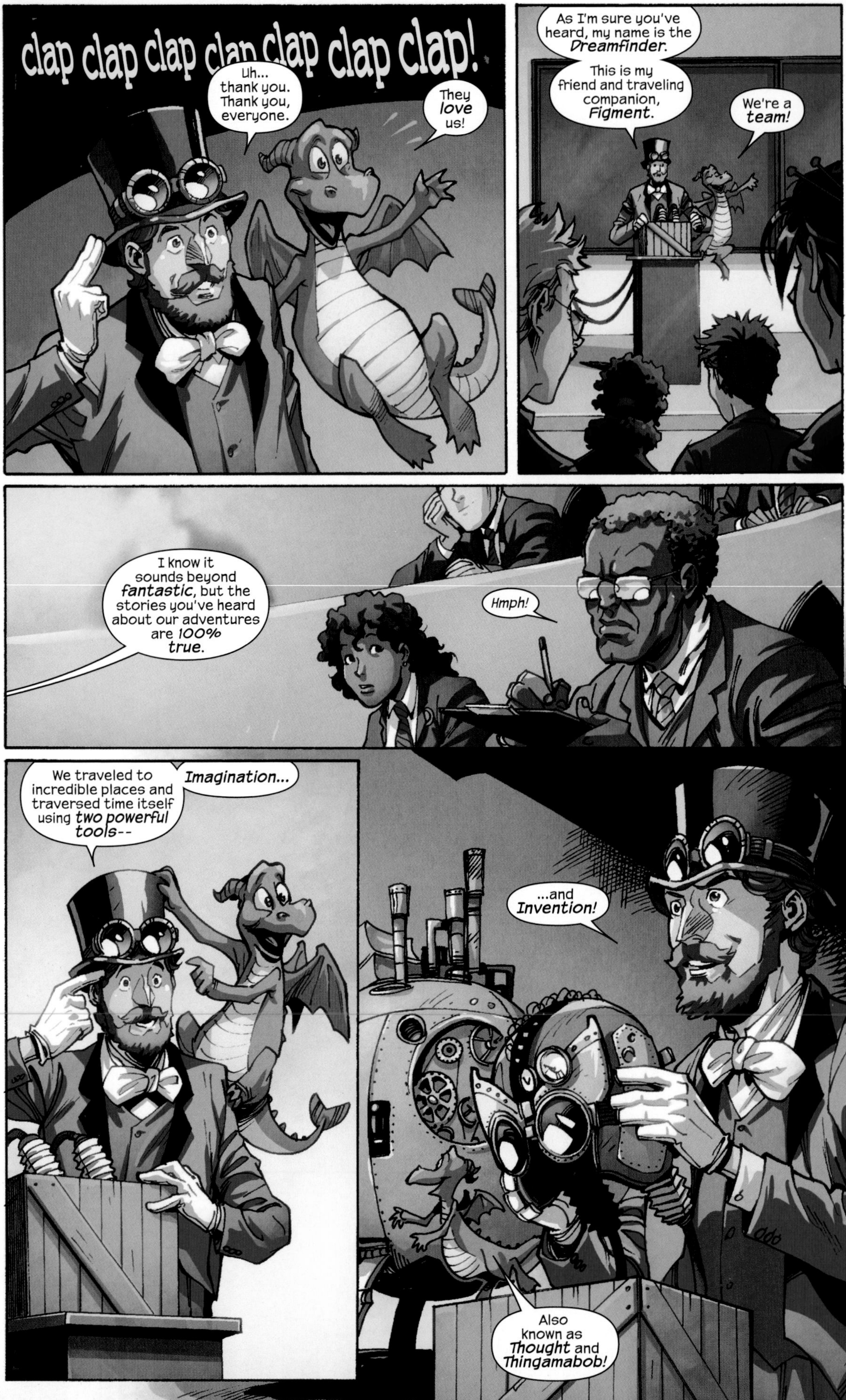
clap clap clap clap clap clap clap!
Uh... thank you. Thank you, everyone.
They love us!
As I'm sure you've heard, my name is the Dreamfinder.
This is my friend and traveling companion, Figment.
We're a team!
I know it sounds beyond fantastic, but the stories you've heard about our adventures are 100% true.
Hmph!
We traveled to incredible places and traversed time itself using two powerful tools--
Imagination...
...and Invention!
Also known as Thought and Thingamabob!

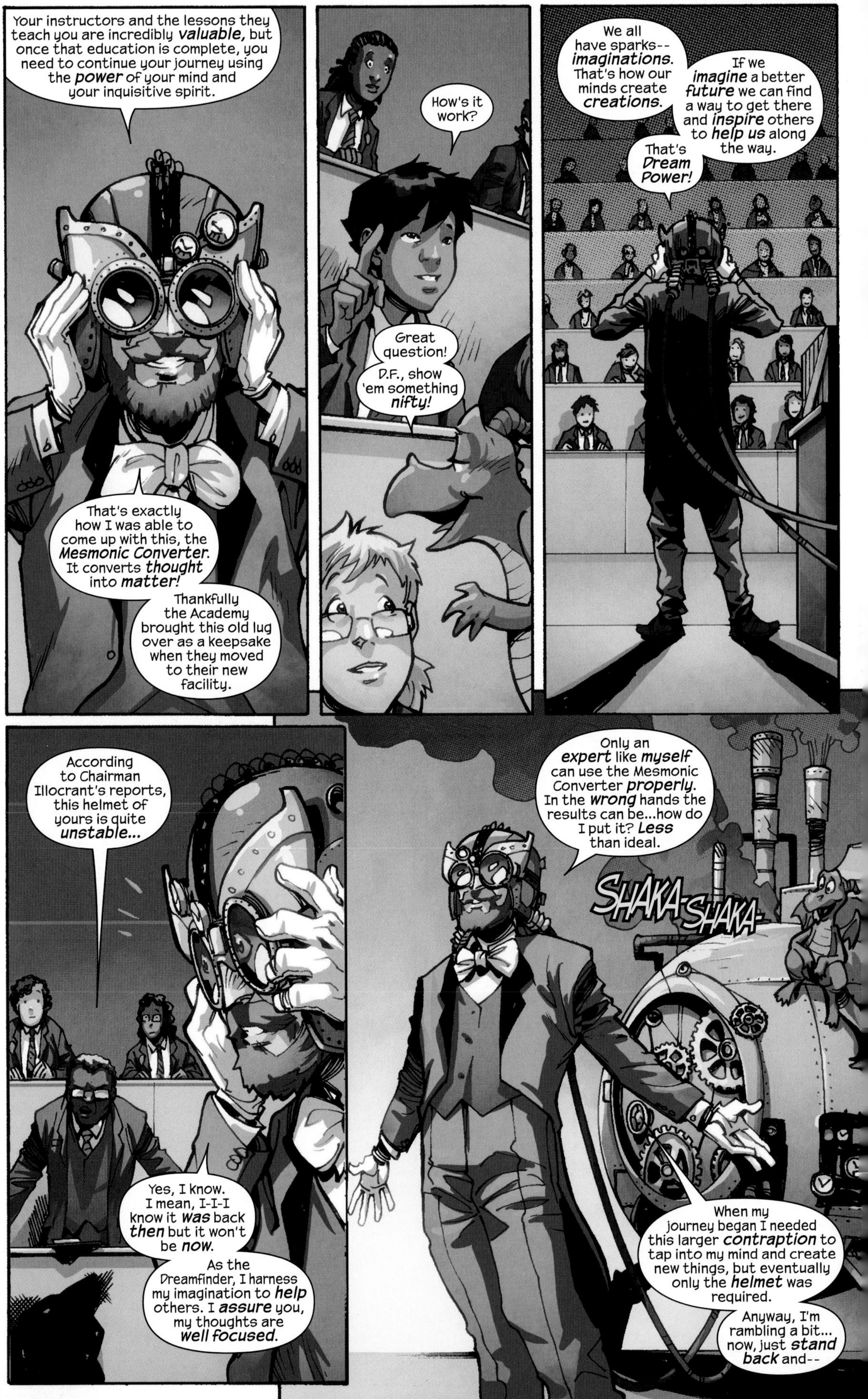
Your instructors and the lessons they teach you are incredibly valuable, but once that education is complete, you need to continue your journey using the power of your mind and your inquisitive spirit.
That's exactly how I was able to come up with this, the Mesmonic Converter. It converts thought into matter!
Thankfully the Academy brought this old lug over as a keepsake when they moved to their new facility.
How's it work?
Great question!
D.F., show 'em something nifty!
We all have sparks--imaginations. That's how our minds create creations.
If we imagine a better future we can find a way to get there and inspire others to help us along the way.
That's Dream Power!
According to Chairman Illocrant's reports, this helmet of yours is quite unstable...
Yes, I know. I mean, I-I-I know it was back then but it won't be now.
As the Dreamfinder, I harness my imagination to help others. I assure you, my thoughts are well focused.
Only an expert like myself can use the Mesmonic Converter properly. In the wrong hands the results can be...how do I put it? Less than ideal.
SHAKA-SHAKA-
When my journey began I needed this larger contraption to tap into my mind and create new things, but eventually only the helmet was required.
Anyway, I'm rambling a bit... now, just stand back and--

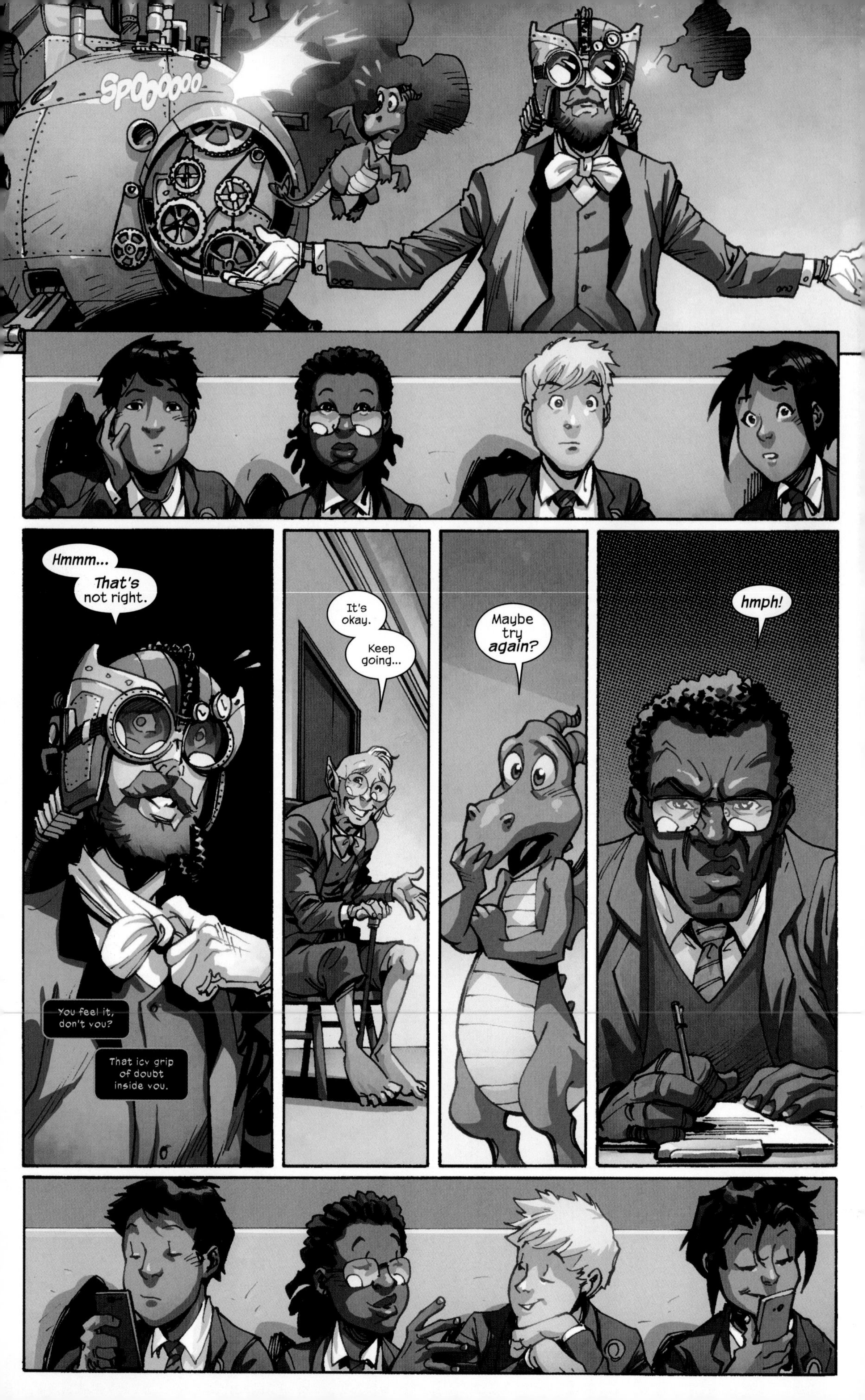
SPOOOOOO
Hmmm... That's not right.
You feel it, don't you?
That icy grip of doubt inside you.
It's okay.
Keep going...
Maybe try again?
hmph!

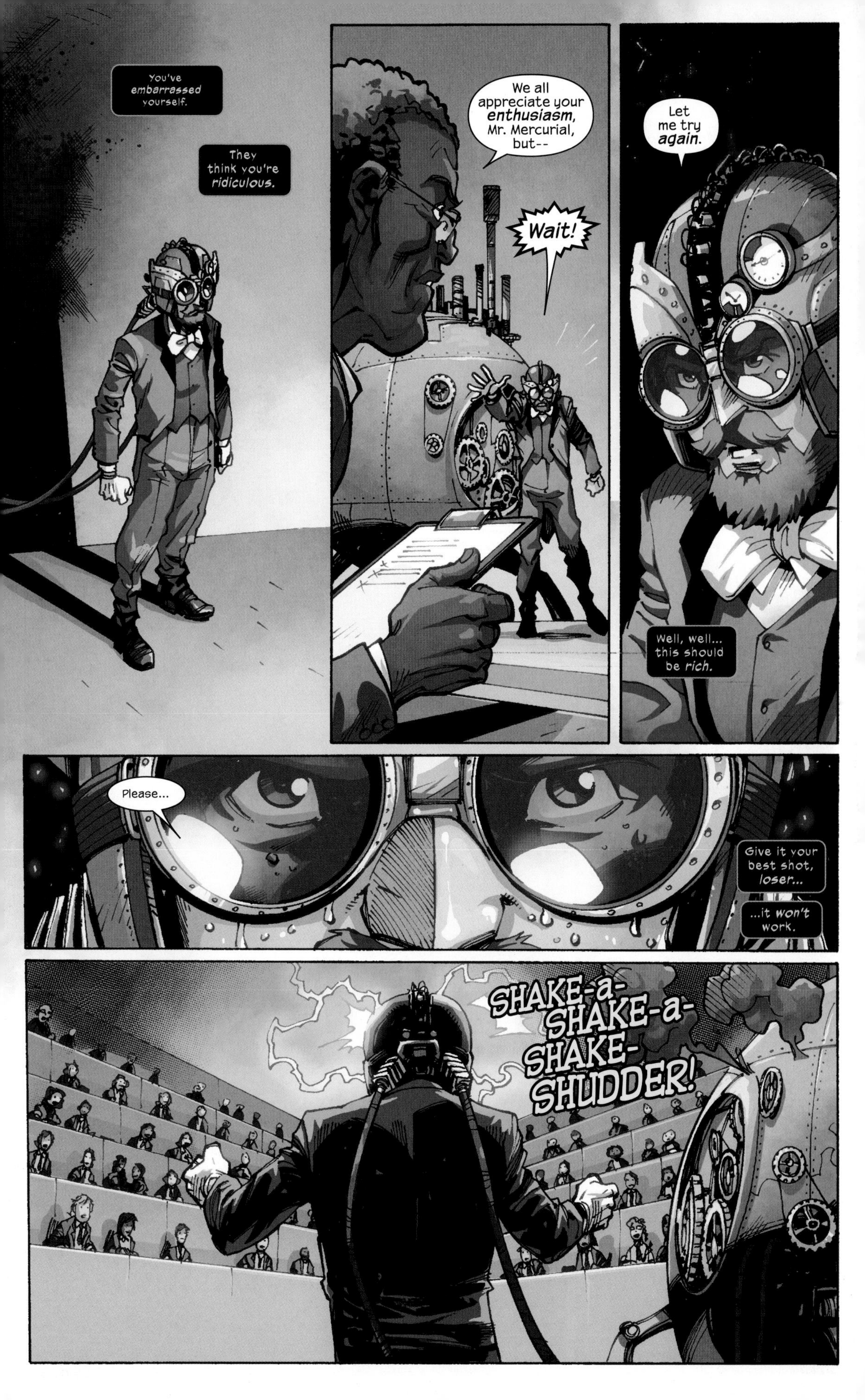
You've embarrassed yourself.
They think you're ridiculous.
We all appreciate your enthusiasm, Mr. Mercurial, but--
Wait!
Let me try again.
Well, well... this should be rich.
Please...
Give it your best shot, loser...
...it won't work.
SHAKE-a-SHAKE-a-SHAKE-SHUDDER!

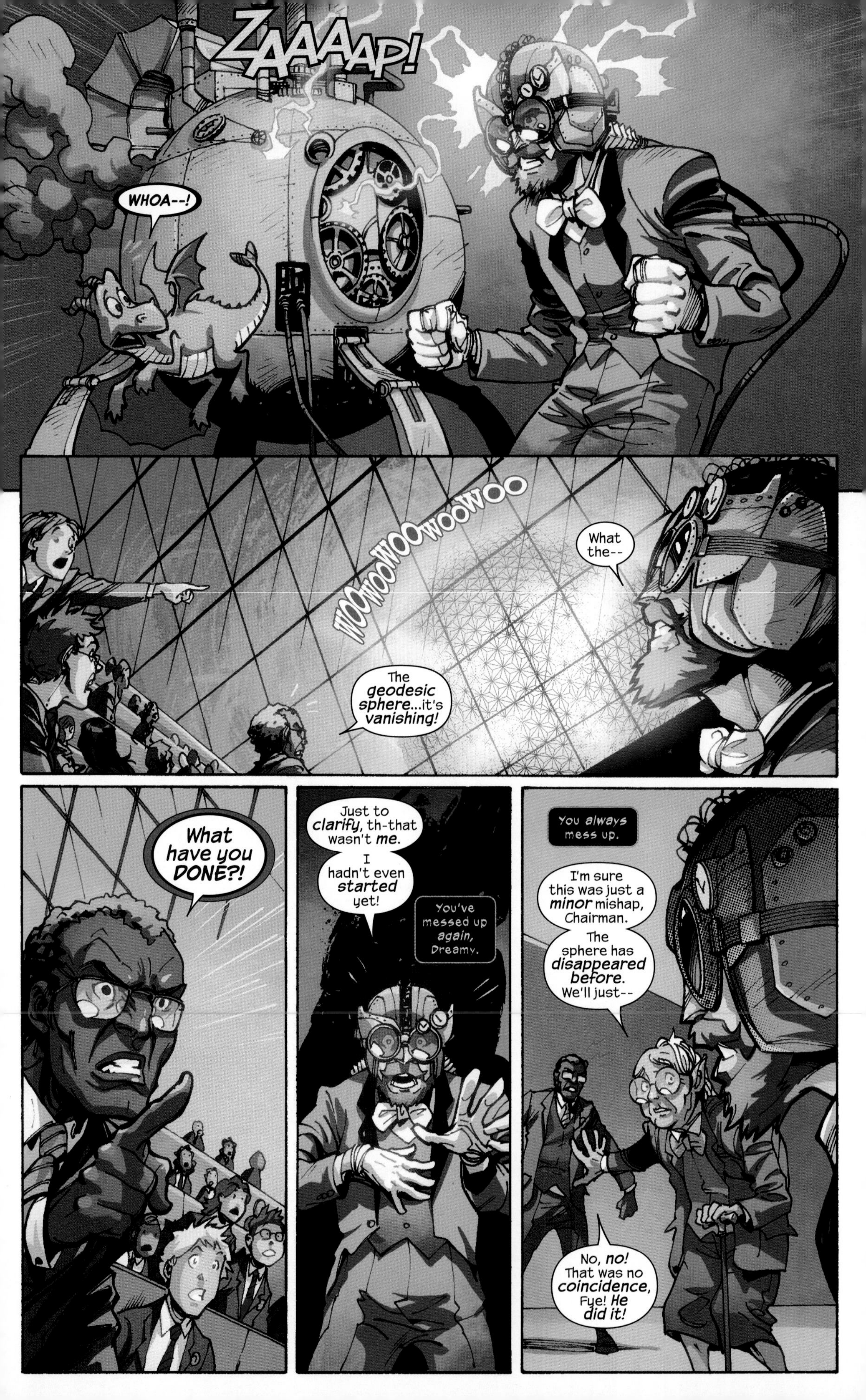
ZAAAAP!
WHOA--!
WOOWOOWOOWOOWOO
What the--
The geodesic sphere...it's vanishing!
What have you DONE?!
Just to clarify, th-that wasn't me.
I hadn't even started yet!
You've messed up again, Dreamy.
You always mess up.
I'm sure this was just a minor mishap, Chairman.
The sphere has disappeared before. We'll just--
No, no! That was no coincidence, Fye! He did it!

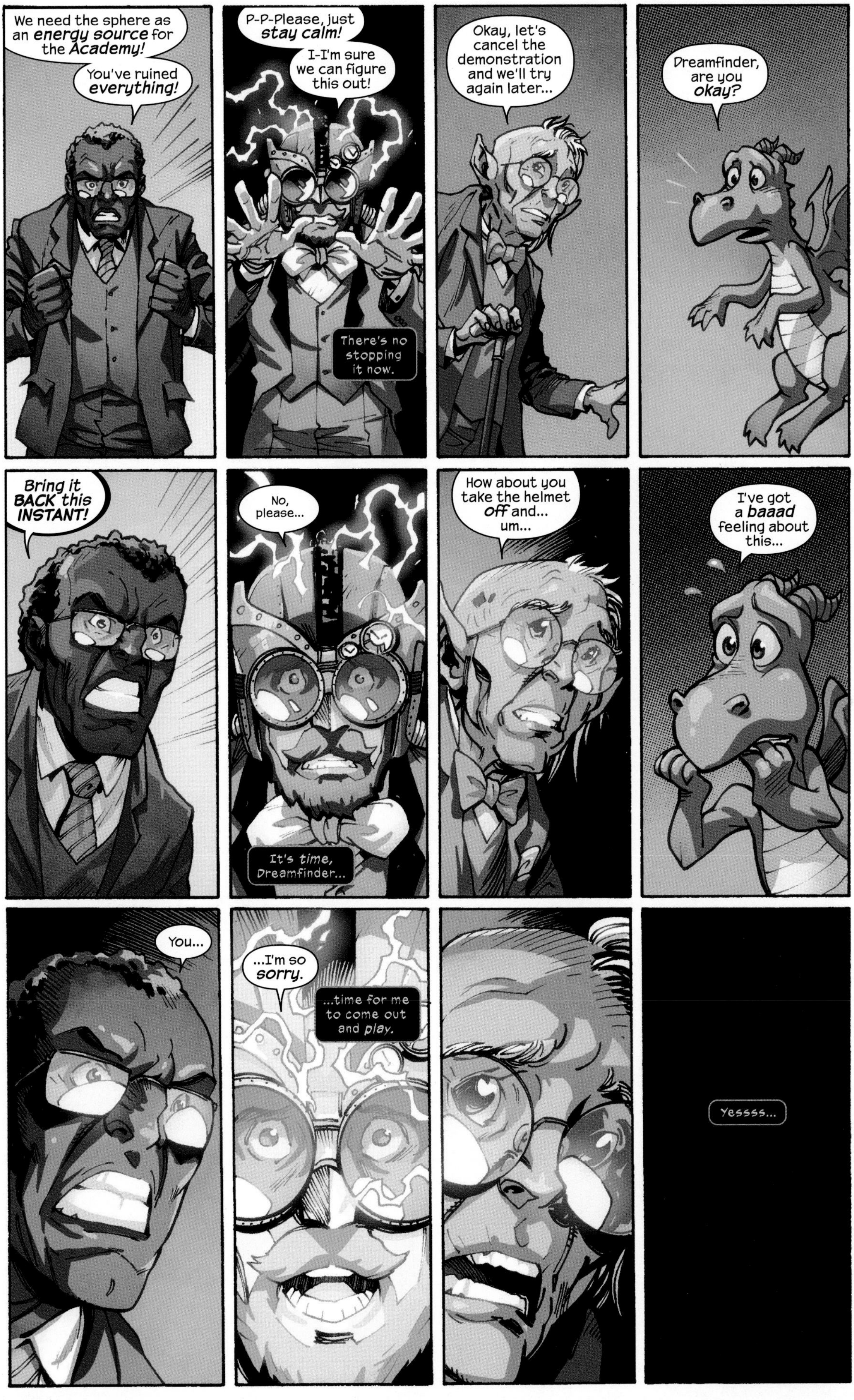
We need the sphere as an *energy source* for the *Academy!*
You've ruined *everything!*
P-P-Please, just *stay calm!*
I-I'm sure we can figure this out!
There's no stopping it now.
Okay, let's cancel the demonstration and we'll try again later...
Dreamfinder, are you *okay?*
Bring it BACK this INSTANT!
No, please...
It's *time,* Dreamfinder...
How about you take the helmet *off* and... um...
I've got a *baaad* feeling about this...
You...
...I'm so *sorry.*
...time for me to come out and *play.*
Yessss...

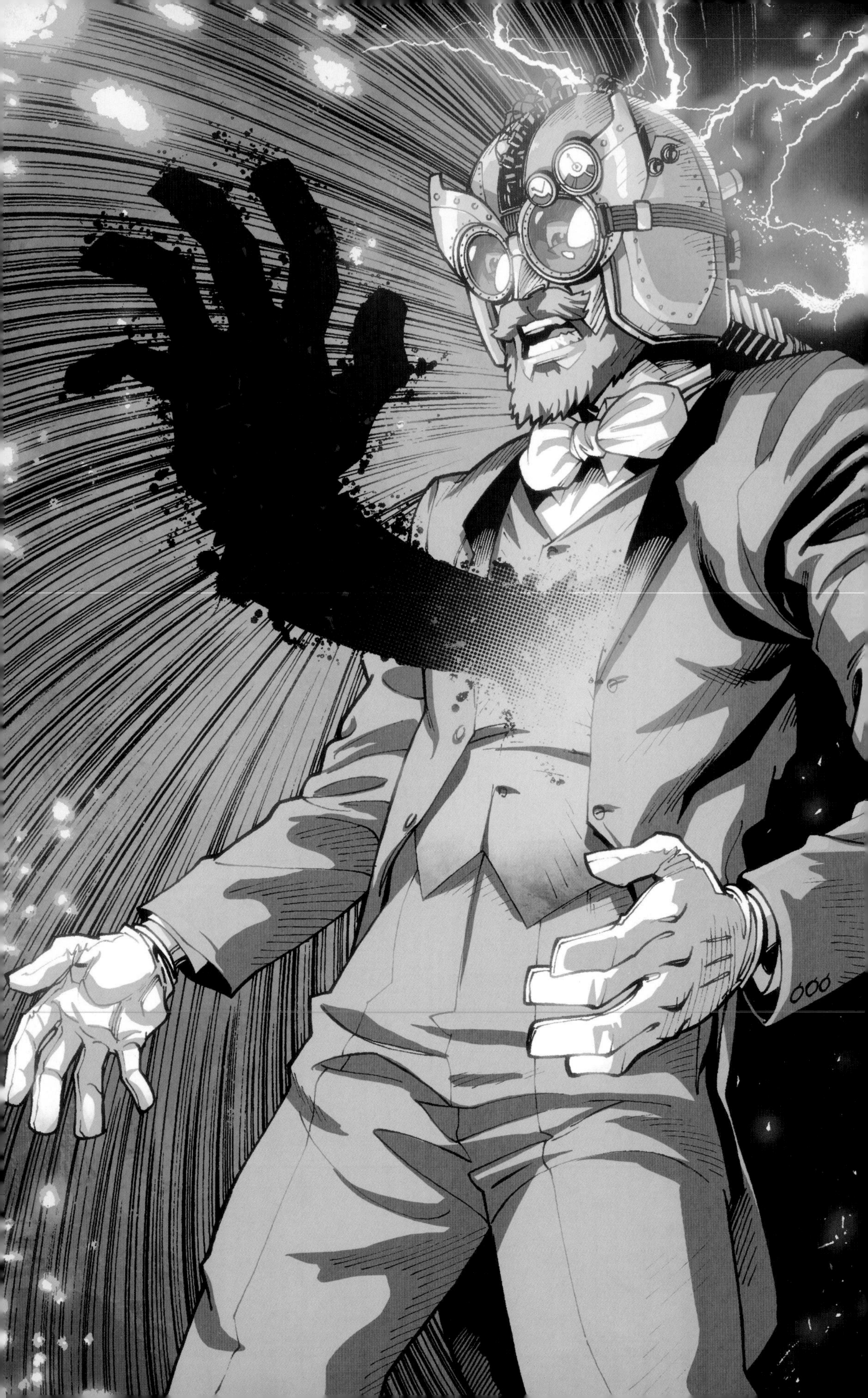

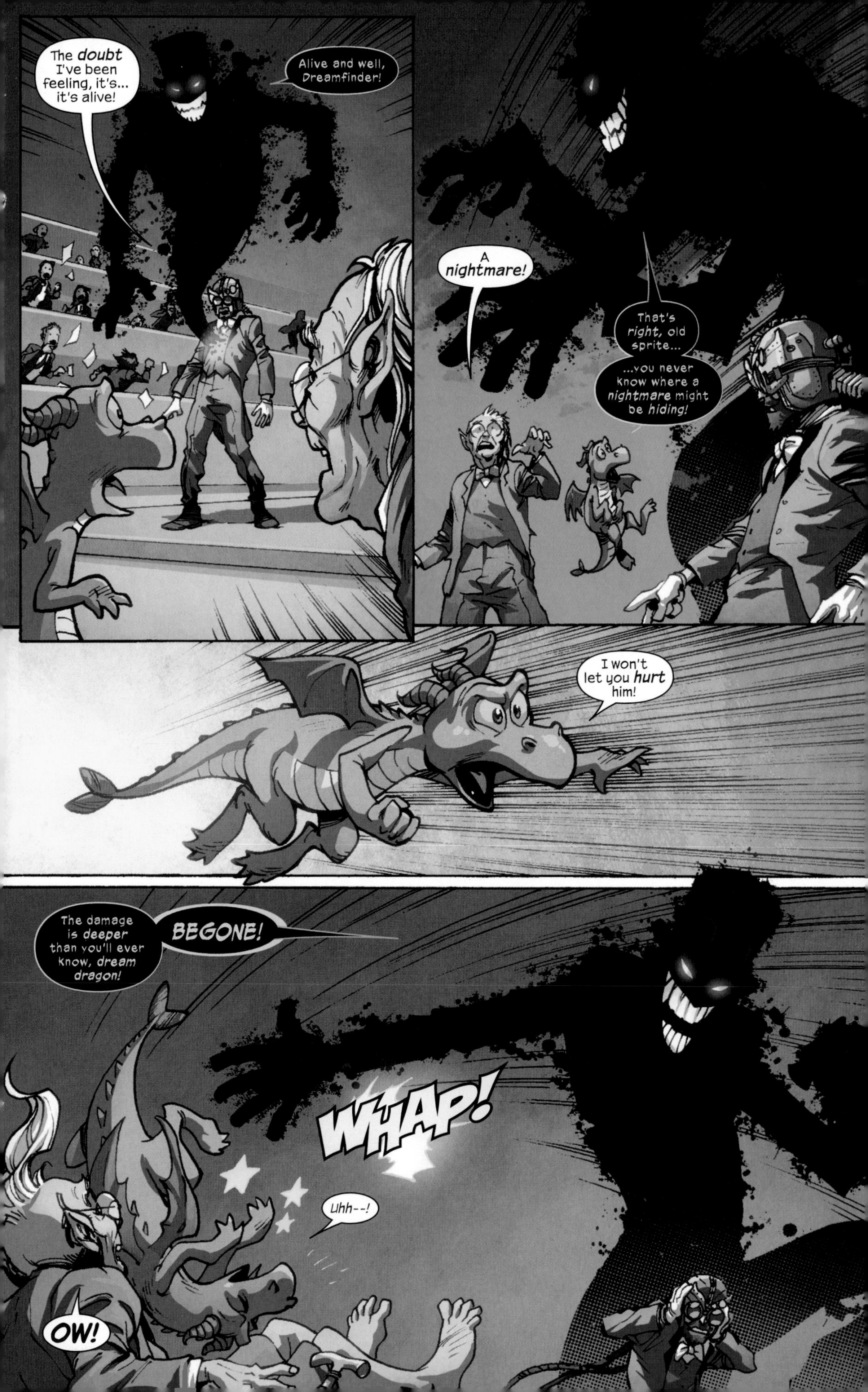

The *doubt* I've been feeling, it's... it's alive!
Alive and well, Dreamfinder!
A *nightmare!*
That's *right,* old sprite...
...you never know where a *nightmare* might be *hiding!*
I won't let you **hurt** him!
BEGONE!
The damage is *deeper* than you'll ever know, *dream dragon!*
WHAP!
Uhh--!
OW!

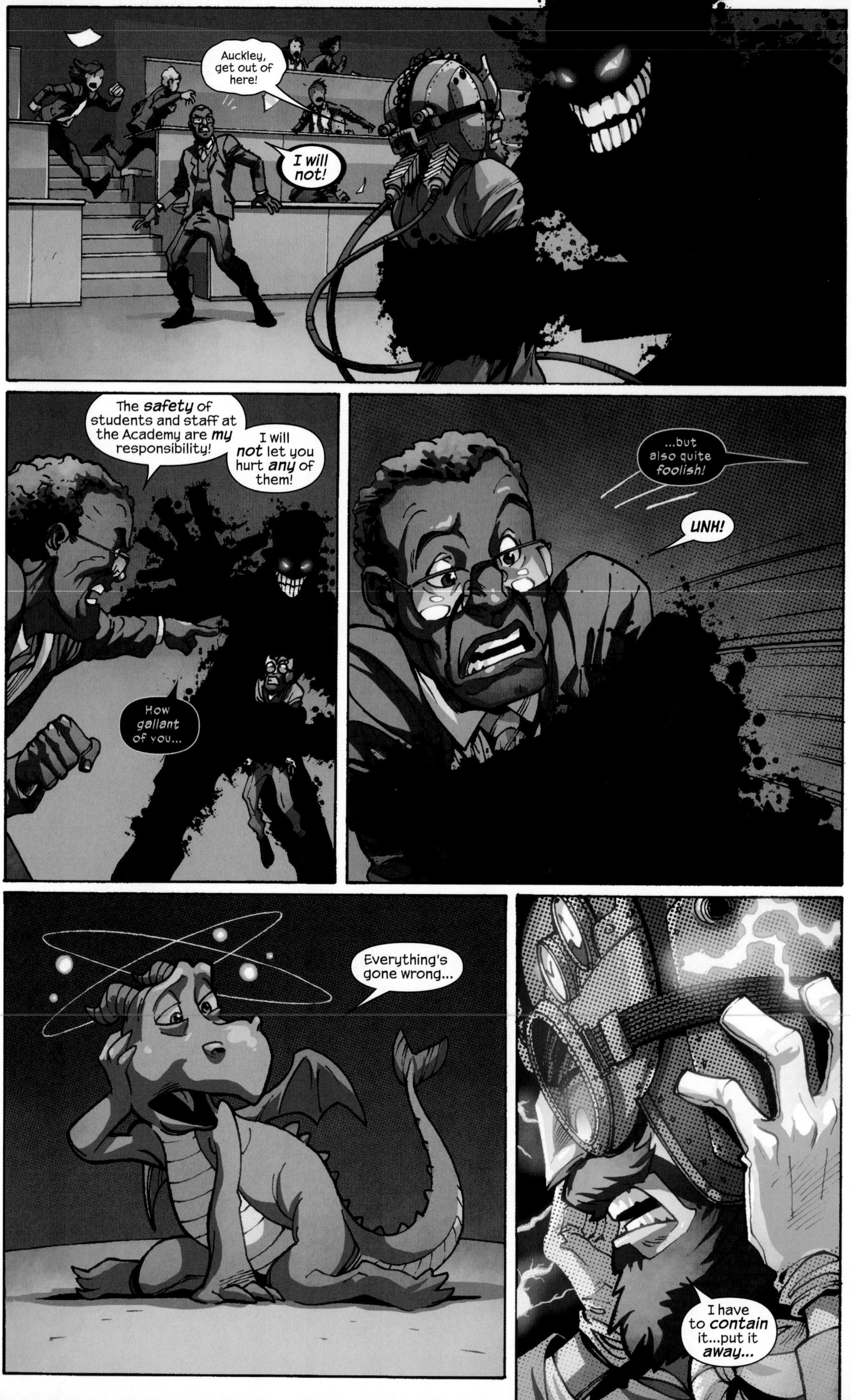
Auckley, get out of here!
I will not!
The safety of students and staff at the Academy are my responsibility!
I will not let you hurt any of them!
How gallant of you...
...but also quite foolish!
UNH!
Everything's gone wrong...
I have to contain it...put it away...

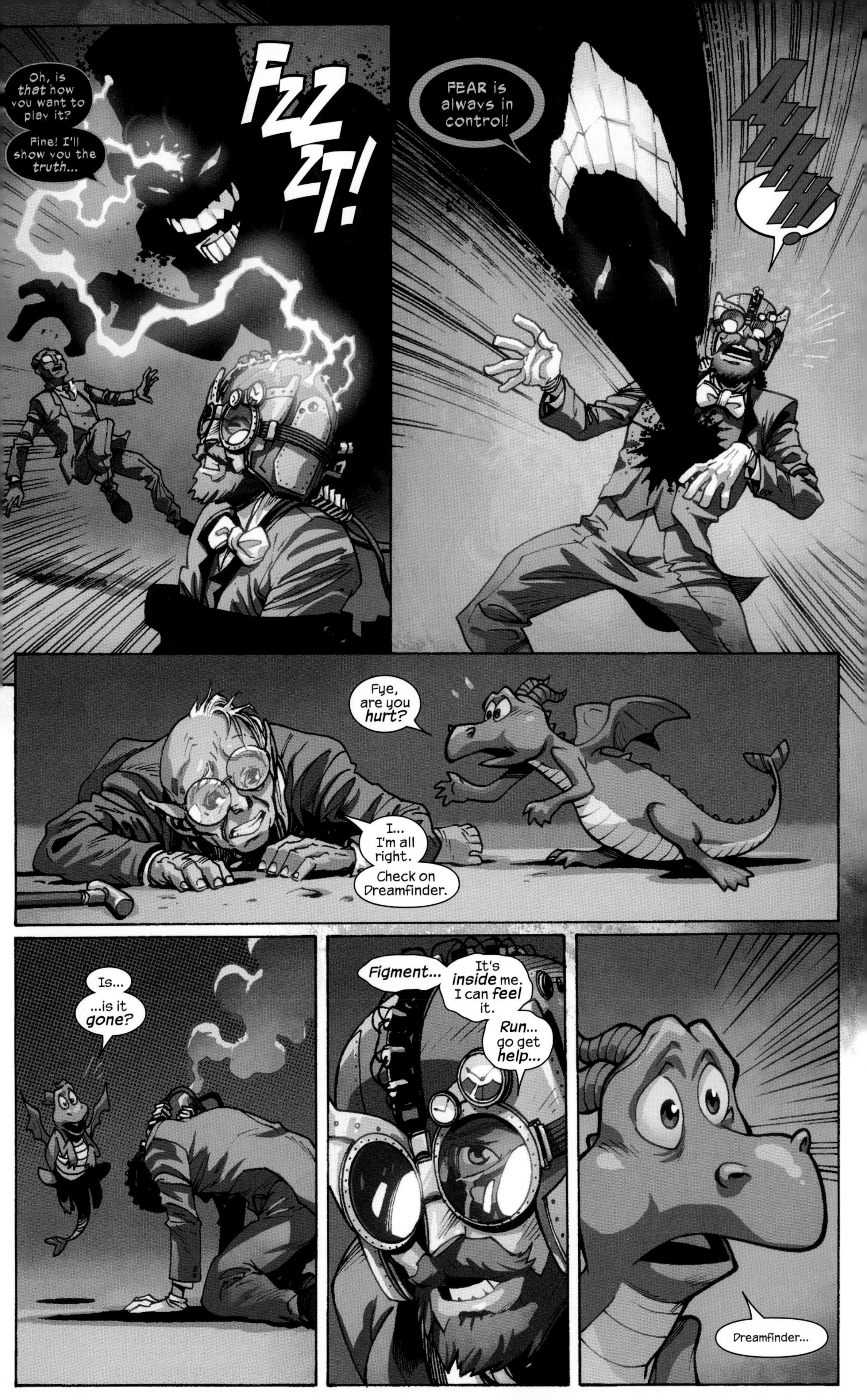
Oh, is *that* how you want to play it?
Fine! I'll show you the *truth*...
FZZZT!
FEAR is always in control!
AHHH!
Fye, are you *hurt?*
I... I'm all right.
Check on Dreamfinder.
Is...
...is it *gone?*
Figment...
It's *inside* me. I can *feel* it.
Run... go get *help...*
Dreamfinder...

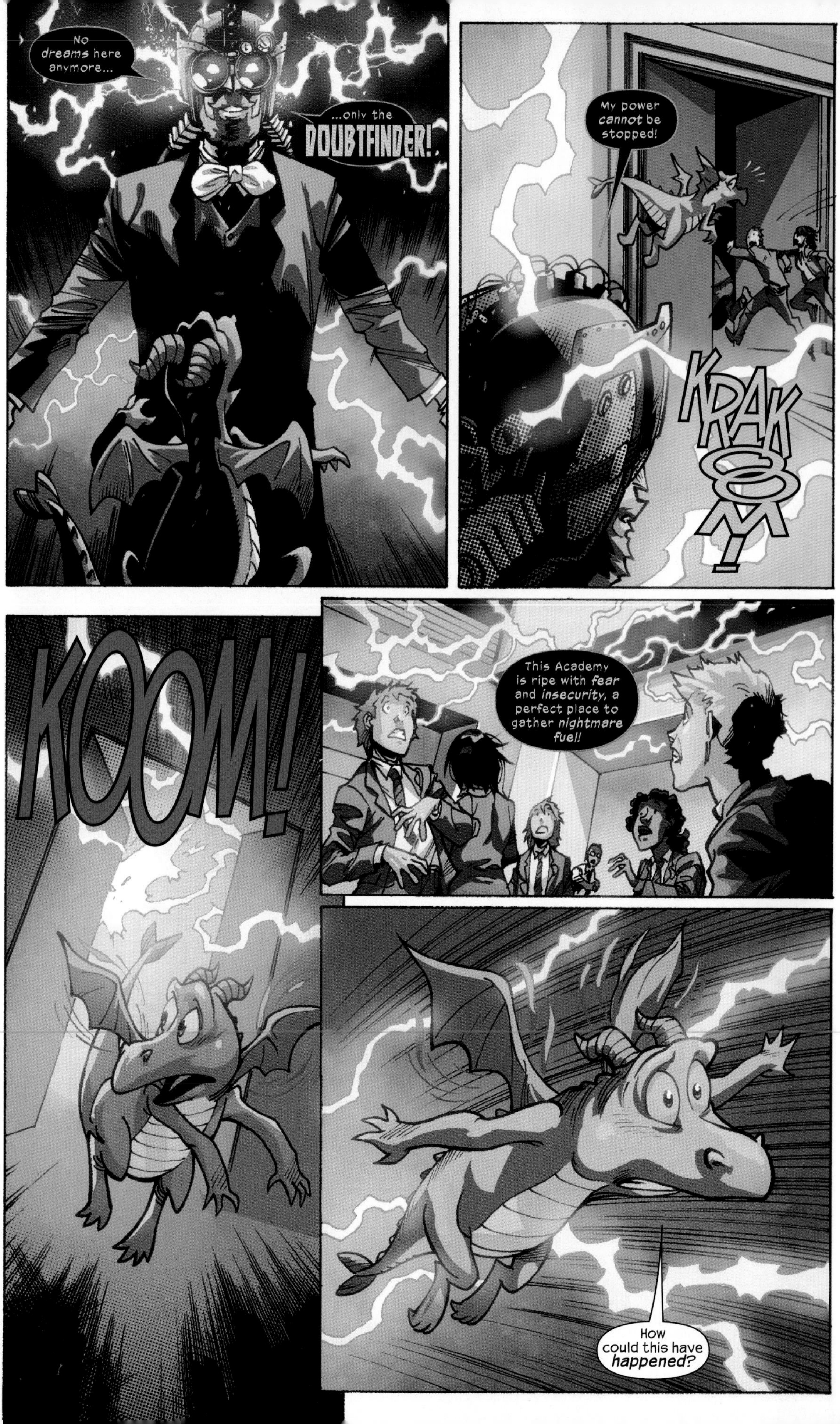
No dreams here anymore...
...only the DOUBTFINDER!
My power cannot be stopped!
KRAKOOM!
KOOM!
This Academy is ripe with fear and insecurity, a perfect place to gather nightmare fuel!
How could this have happened?

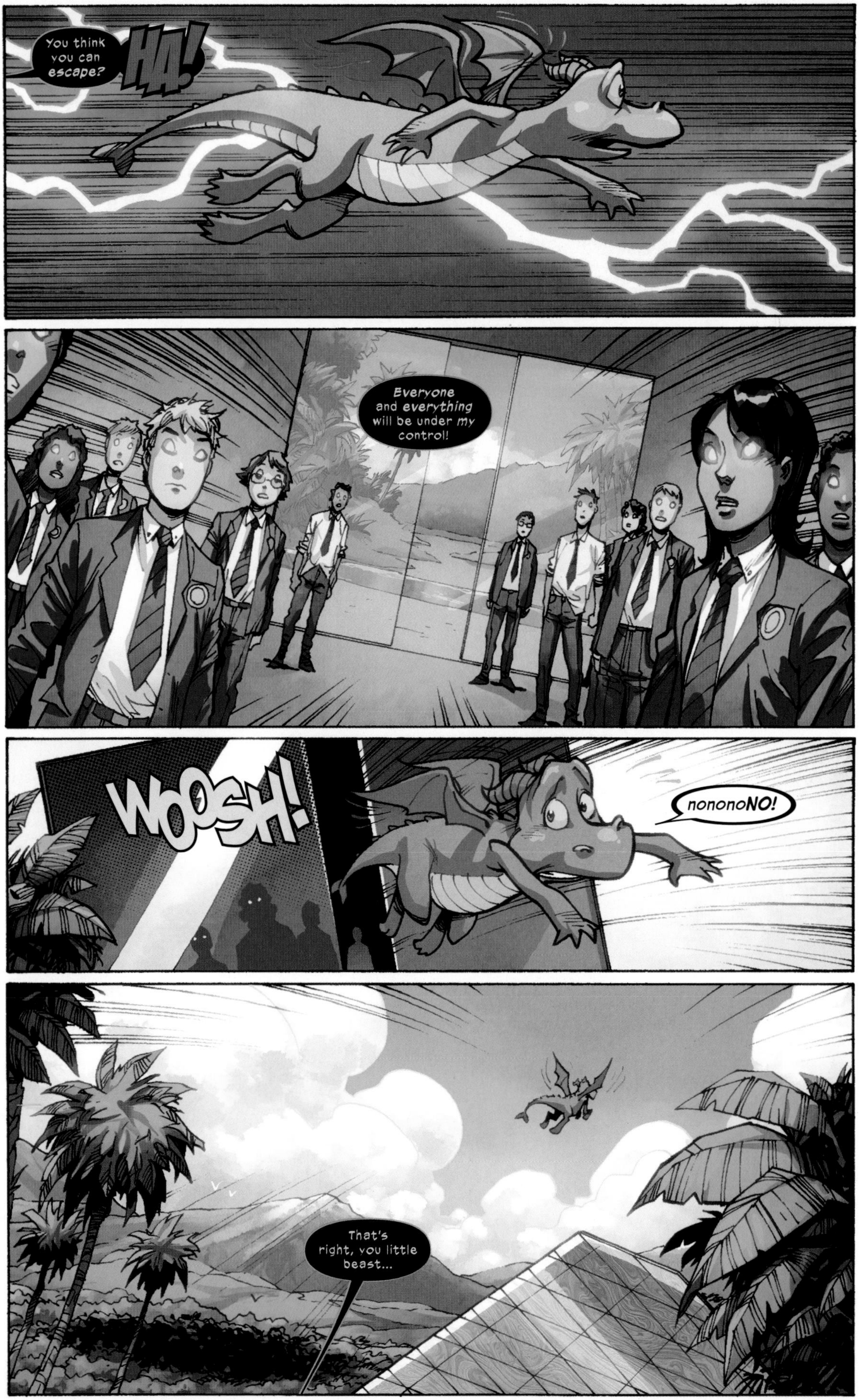
You think you can escape?
HA!
Everyone and everything will be under my control!
WOOSH!
nononoNO!
That's right, you little beast...

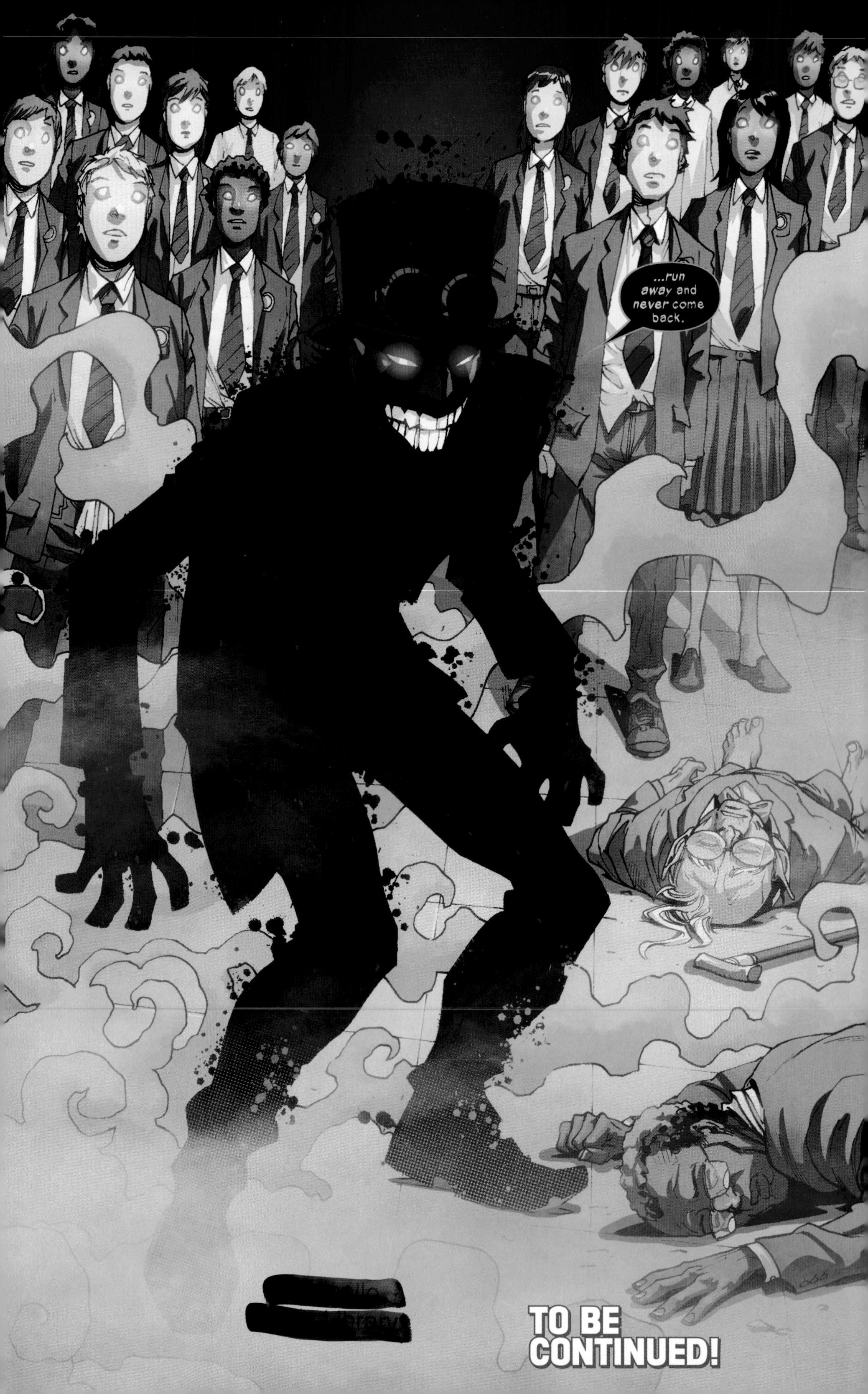
...run away and never come back.
[redacted]
TO BE CONTINUED!